D0316532

This Little Tiger book belongs to:

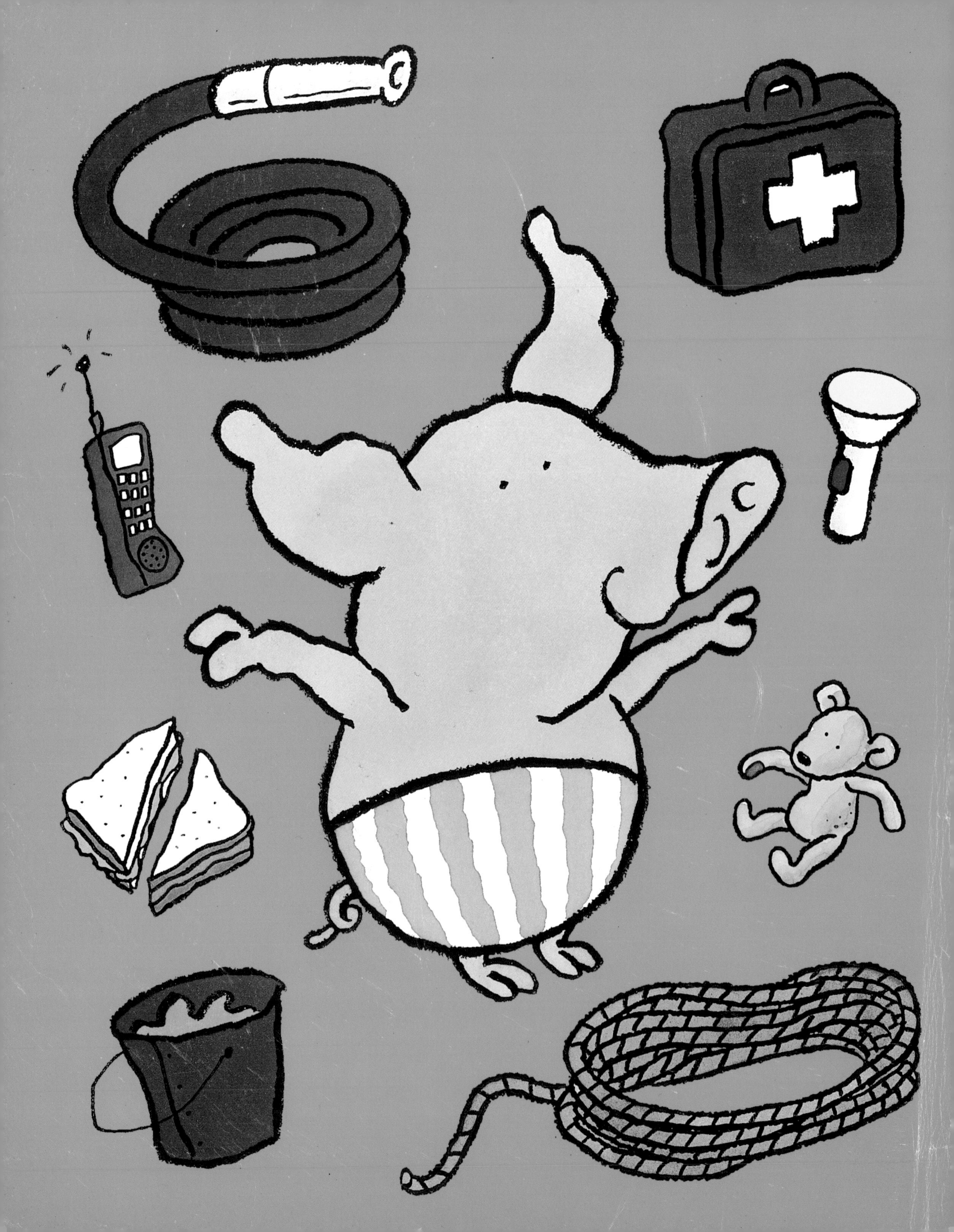

For Harvey

LITTLE TIGER PRESS
An imprint of Magi Publications
1 The Coda Centre, 189 Munster Road, London SW6 6AW
This paperback edition published 2001
First published in Great Britain 2001
2001 © Diane and Christyan Fox
Diane and Christyan Fox have asserted their rights to
be identified as the author and illustrator of this work
under the Copyright, Designs and Patents Act, 1988.
Printed in Singapore • All rights reserved
ISBN 1 85430 698 7
3 5 7 9 10 8 6 4 2

Fireman PiggyWiggy

Christyan and Diane Fox

LITTLE TIGER PRESS

Whenever I see a fire engine racing by, I dream of all the things that I would do if I were a fearless fireman...

RRRRIIINNGGG...

I would wear
a big yellow hat
and slide down
a shiny pole
on my way to
an emergency...

and ride around in
with a flashing light

a big red fire engine
and a screaming siren.

Maybe I would climb a tall ladder to rescue someone stuck in a very high place...

or save
someone
stuck down
a deep
dark hole.

I could even cool everyone down on a hot sunny day...

and put out
with my
water

blazing fires
powerful
hose.

But it's always that in a real

good to know emergency...

I can call a real life fearless fireman who will come racing to the rescue.

Escape into a world of books...

For information regarding any of the above titles or for our catalogue, please contact: Little Tiger Press, 1 The Coda Centre, 189 Munster Road, London SW6 6AW, UK
Telephone: 020 7385 6333 Fax: 020 7385 7333 e-mail: info@littletiger.co.uk